Hannah Flagg Gould

Hymns and Other Poems for Children

Hannah Flagg Gould

Hymns and Other Poems for Children

ISBN/EAN: 9783744779388

Printed in Europe, USA, Canada, Australia, Japan

Cover: Foto ©Andreas Hilbeck / pixelio.de

More available books at **www.hansebooks.com**

HYMNS

AND

OTHER POEMS

FOR

CHILDREN.

BY HANNAH F. GOULD.

WITH ILLUSTRATIONS.

PUBLISHED BY

ALLEN BROTHERS,

NEW YORK.

1869.

CONTENTS.

CONTENTS.

HYMNS

OTHER POEMS

FOR CHILDREN.

DAY HYMN.

WHEN morn hath round our pillow shed
   Her pure and precious light,
We must not idly keep our bed,
   That gave us rest by night.
We must arise our God to praise,
   Who kept us while we lay ;
And ask his care through all the ways
   He marks for us by day.

When, shining in his noontide power,
   We see the golden sun,
We should review each by-gone hour
   Of day, for what we've done.
We should aspire our hearts to lift
   His glorious height above ;
And from our Maker seek the gift
   Of sun-like truth and love.

When falling shades and evening dew
  The earth in silence veil,
We should to Him our prayer renew
  Whose mercies never fail!
We must in God fold up our hearts
  Ere slumber seal our eyes;
And trust -- when sleep at morn departs,
  In him to wake and rise.

STAR HYMN.

From its home so high and far,
There's a little twinkling star,
Down through evening shades and damp,
Beaming, like a diamond lamp!

Soft as angel ministry
Doth its lustre come to me;
While to God, who holds it there,
I address my soul in prayer.

Clouds may rise and intervene
Me and that dear star between;

While, unchanged, the star will be
True to heaven, and true to me.

Sinful thoughts may thus arise
In my soul, and o'er my eyes
Bring a vapor, that will hide
God's bright angel at my side!

May the penitential tear
Then my clouded vision clear,
And my drooping spirit feel
Christ apply the pardon-seal!

Now that peaceful star on high,
Like an angel watcher's eye,
Do I love to know will keep
Beaming o'er me while I sleep.

LITTLE FRIENDS OF JESUS.

Young children sang "Hosanna!"
Where Jesus drew the throng;
The palm-branch was their banner,
And angels taught their song.

Those little prompt believers
  In Christ, their Lord and King,
Were of the first receivers
  Of joy he came to bring.

And their sweet infant story,
  That now so fresh appears,
Has given their Savior glory
  These eighteen hundred years.
Whilst they the palm-branch bearing,
  When Christ on earth was found,
Bright crowns in Heaven are wearing,
  And sing his throne around.

Though there his brightness falleth
  On saint and seraphim,
On earth he sweetly calleth
  The little ones to him.
He loves the hearts of childhood
  Made his by faith and prayer ;
As we, from heath and wild wood
  Love flowers for our parterre.

Each gift — each word that's spoken
  To spread his kingdom here,

He treasures as a token
  Of love to him sincere.
And, little sons and daughters
  Of happy Christian land,
Know ye, beyond the waters,
  What heathen idols stand?

There heathen children never
  The name of Jesus heard!
They have no hope forever,
  Unless they learn his word.
If yours be love's confidings
  In him, his love proclaim:
Send out the glorious tidings
  Of life in Jesus' name.

'Twill, as your signal palmy,
  Be witnessed from on high,
And yield an unction balmy
  To souls that else would die.
O, send the heavenly manna,
  The "bread of life" to them,
That they may sing "Hosanna"
  In New Jerusalem.

THE SABBATH.

Day of days, the dearest, best;
Hallowed by Jehovah's rest!
When his six day's work was done,
Holy rose the seventh sun.

When creation's pillars stood,
And the Lord pronounced them good,
Morning stars together sang—
Heaven with sabbath praises rang.

Earth in pristine beauty shone,
Like a gem, before his throne,
While he marked thee as his claim,
And baptized thee with his name.

Choice of God, thou blessed day!
At thy dawn the grave gave way
To the power of him within,
Who had, sinless, bled for sin.

Thine the radiance to illume
First, for man, the dismal tomb,
When its bars their weakness owned,
There revealing death dethroned.

Then the "Sun of Rightcousness,"
Rose a darkened world to bless,
Bringing up from mortal night,
Immortality and light.

THE GOLDEN MINSTREL.

Where, from thousand honey-springs,
  Opening blossoms feed the bee,
Some melodious warbler sings,
  Bosomed deep in yonder tree.

On the breeze the music floats
  With the perfume of the flower,
Pouring forth in mellow notes
  From the lovely minstrel's bower.

'Mid the leaves and clustered bloom,
  Where to shroud his dress he stole,
Now appears his golden plume ;
  'Tis a brilliant Oriole.

Little jewel! hidden there,
  Still he had remained concealed,
Had not that mellifluous air
  Thus his covert form revealed.

Not to win himself a name
  Would he so his powers display;
Nor to swell a creature's fame;
  'Tis to God he pours the lay.

Oft it seems as if the birds
  Came with lessons sweet to man;
That to pure, unwritten words
  Their delicious music ran.

Ever seem they to rejoice,
  In the sunshine, or the showers;
Gratitude attunes their voice
  Unto Him who gave their powers.

Under blue or sombre sky,
  On the bough or in the dust,
They've a bright and cheerful eye,
  And a heart of truth and trust.

In his leafy, calm retreat,
  Like a happy human soul
Singing at its Father's feet,
  Is the lovely Oriole.

Sweet as incense up the skies,
Welcome to his Maker's ear,
Roll the artless melodies
From the little warbler here.

SABBATH SCHOOL HYMN.

Our Father, who art throned above,
As heaven's eternal king,
So high! thou still from earth dost love
The praise a child may sing.

Then lend, we pray, a listening ear,
Whilst we, an infant throng,
Unite our feeble voices here
To lift the grateful song!

We bless thee for thy goodness known;
We bless thee for our trust,
That still thou'lt guard us from thy throne,
Though we are in the dust.

With thanks for all thy kindness, Lord,
We give thee highest praise,
That we possess thy sacred Word,
And holy Sabbath days.

A Savior by that blessed Book
We find, who loved us so,
He laid his glory by, and took
An infant's form below!

He died but for the sins of those
Who'd be through him forgiven:
Then on the Sabbath morn he rose
To lead our hearts to Heaven.

GOD IN THE THUNDER STORM.

"The God of glory thundereth."—Ps. xxix: 3.

When peals the thunder long and loud,
The Lord is speaking from the cloud.
Whilst they who know him not, may fear,
His children love his voice to hear.
And though it sound in noise and storm,
His love but takes the varied form;
To give them purer vital breath,
"The God of glory thundereth."

When lightnings flash from out the sky,
It is the Lord who passeth by,

With brightness from his holy throne,
In gleamings on his raiment shown.
His splendor may the sinner awe ;
But they who know and love his law,
Recall his Word of life, that saith
" The God of glory thundereth."

At last, when scenes of life shall end,
And Christ arrayed in power descend ;
His voice will rend the silent tomb ;
His lightnings every eye relume !
His friends, in that august review,
Will shine with joy his friends anew ;
While, with the keys of life and death,
" The God of glory thundereth."

THE LAD WITH THE LOAVES AND FISHES.

" There is a lad here, which hath five barley loaves and two small fishes." — St. John, vi: 9

When by Christ the throng were led
Up the lonely mountain's side,
Where the multitude were fed,
Who the wondrous food supplied ?

B

Those *five loaves* and *fishes two*,
Which for thousands were to do —
Who the loaves and fishes brought
Whence the miracle was wrought?

Wife, nor maid, nor mother then
    Might the rural feast prepare ;
Not the young, nor white-haired men
    Should provide the timely fare.
But a little Christian boy
For the work did Christ employ,
Pleased, his host of friends among,
To distinguish one so young.

Still doth Jesus love to count
    Young disciples, fair and true,
Like the lad upon the mount
    Where his early friends he drew.
Every little gift or deed
He can bless, like planted seed,
Or the barley-loaves of old,
To increase a thousand fold.

Though your gift be but a mite
    Spared to send his word afar,

It may prove a ray of light
  Spread and brightened to a star!
This the star of morn may be
O'er some land beyond the sea,
Opening up the shining way
Of the peaceful gospel day.

Little friends of Jesus, aim,
  While your life is in the flower,
With his spirit, in his name,
  To commend his love and power.
Emulate the Hebrew lad,
Who, imparting what he had,
Saw the wonders Christ could do,
And the moral left to you

EMMA'S DREAM.

My little contribution,
  With ready heart and hand,
I gave, to send the Word of God
  To distant heathen land:
And ere I went to rest that night,
  I kneeled to God in prayer,
That he would change my gift to light
  For souls in darkness there.

When I was lost in slumber,
  There seemed just o'er my bed,
An angel child, with beaming brow
  And shining wings out-spread ;
And stainless seemed the robe to flow
  About that lovely one,

As lies a glowing sheet of snow
  Beneath the morning sun.

A touch of golden glory
  Was on her wavy hair ;
Her face, with rose-tint on the cheek,
  Was like the lily fair.
And oh ! she sang a holy song,
  Which angels only know
To sound in their adoring throng ;
  And never learnt below !

She told a hasty story
  About her life on earth,
When here a little dark Hindoo,
  Of distant Indian birth ;
That once her parents were of those
  Who God in Ganges deem,
Where oft her babe the mother throws,
  An offering, on the stream :

But when the missions taught them
  To read the WORD, and pray
To God in Heaven, through Jesus' name,
  Their gods were cast away ;

That e'er she died, she loved to sing
  How Christ for her could die :
And then he gave her spirit wing
  To soar to him on high.

I drew my breath, to ask her
  About the joys above ;
When silently she disappeared,
  With parting smile of love !
Awaking then, I prayed for more
  That I might send away
To shed upon some heathen shore
  The beams of gospel day.

THE LITTLE CAKE; A SCRIPTURE STORY.

When o'er ancient Israel,
Ahab reigned, with Jezebel,
Fearful things the land befell,
  From their pagan sway :
Prophets of the Lord were slain ;
Altars reared to idols vain ;

Sins were known, to earth a stain
Never washed away.

Ahab's bold Zidonian wife
Still pursued the vengeful strife,
Thirsting for Elijah's life,
    Whom the Lord had sent,
On the land denouncing woe
Which the king and queen would show,
For the blood they'd caused to flow,
    What his threatenings meant.

But the way the Prophet took,
Shown of God, to Cherith brook,
Where, in secret cave or nook,
    He pursuit would shun.
Ravens, as the Lord had said,
Daily then, with meat and bread,
Night and morning came and fed
    There, the lonely one.

Ministers of God were they,
Wafting on their airy way
Food his servant's life to stay
    In his drear retreat;

Till, as he had prophesied,
Dew and rain to earth denied
Scared the grass, the streamlets dried,
    As by torrid heat.

He who once a world could drown,
Now upon his foes sent down
Drought and famine, in his frown,
    Through the kingdom spread.
Flock and herd, for drink and feed,
Pined and died on hill and mead ;
Man, too, fell, for broke indeed
    Was his staff of bread.

From his covert sad and low,
God then bade Elijah go,
On a way that he would show,
    And protect his path.
Rough the road he traveled o'er,
Till a gate he stood before
Near a widow's humble door,
    Down in Zarephath.

She was out, and looking round,
Picking fuel from the ground,

When she heard the startling sound
  Of the stranger's feet.
" Give me drink," Elijah said,
" And a morsel of your bread ;
  Ere my fainting life hath fled,
    Let me drink and eat ! "

" As the Lord doth live," quoth she,
" For my famished son and me,
  In our keen necessity,
    Only left have I
Little oil, and meal to make
For us twain a little cake,
Which I gather sticks to bake,
    That we eat, and die ! "

Still the Prophet urged his plea,
" Water bring, and bread, to me ;
  Haste with these ! and then for thee
    And thy son provide."
Quick the cup his thirst to slake
Then she brought ; she sped to bake ;
And the ready little cake
    Soon his want supplied.

From that hour her care had ceased ;
She, from want and fear released,
Saw her meal and oil increased ;
   Ever full, her store.
God, who saw her feeling heart,
Trustful, void of self and art,
Prompt her morsel to impart,
   Blessed her evermore.

Holy men, on heathen ground,
Now the Gospel trump would sound
More, could means of life be found
   For their distant way.
But the needful *little cake* —
Who for this the price will take
From his store, for Jesus' sake,
   Trusting God for pay ?

THE DYING CHILD'S REQUEST.

A little boy, laid sick and low,
   Looked up with languid eye,
And spake as one who seemed to know
   He now was called to die.

He said, "Dear mother, do not grieve
That I must leave you here ;
For you, and every friend I leave,
Will then be doubly dear.

"There's something tells me I must go
Where Christ prepares a home,
To which you all, left now below,
In little while shall come.

"To brother — sister — playmates too,
Some gift I'd leave behind,
To keep me, when I've passed from view,
Still present to their mind.

"You'll thus to them my books divide,
My playthings give away ;
So they'll remember how I died,
When not so old as they.

"Then from my money-box you'll take
The little coins within,
To use as means, for Jesus' sake,
In turning souls from sin.

"'Twould make the heavenly hosts rejoice,
And sing to Jesus' name,

To hear some little heathen's voice
His saving love proclaim.

"My breath is faint — I'm dark and chill;
Soft wings seem hovering nigh:
Come, all, and promise me, you still
Will love me, if I die.

"Oh, mother! tell me — what is this?
Your forms I cannot see!
Come, each, and warm me with a kiss;
The angels bend for me!"

The morning sun shone in, to light
The chamber where he lay;
The soul that made that form so bright,
To Heaven had passed away.

THE HILL-SIDE FLOWER.

Flower upon the green hill-side,
Thou, to shun the threatening blast,
In the grass thy head dost hide,
By the tempest overpast.

Then to greet the azure skies,
  And to feel the soothing sun,
Brighter — sweeter — dost thou rise!
  Tell me, flower, how this is done!

"I will tell thee, as a friend,
  Artless — timid — whispering low;
At the blast 'tis good to bend!
  He who made me, taught me so.

"While his teaching I obey,
  I but fall to rise, and stand,
Brighter for the stormy day,
  Leaning on his viewless hand.

"When to him I've lowly bowed,
  He with freshness fills my cup
From the angry, scowling cloud;
  Gently then he lifts me up.

"So I sink, — and so I rise —
  In the dark or sunny hour,
Minding him who rules the skies : —
  He's my God; and I'm his flower! '

JUVENILE MISSIONARY HYMN.

[Written for a sewing-circle of little girls, preparing articles for an annual sale ; the proceeds of which were for the support of two African children.]

"Come over here and help us!"
    That Macedonian cry,
From dusky Afric do we hear ;
    Nor can our aid deny.
We 'll send our angel, Charity,
    Beyond the deep to sow :
As mustard seed our gift may be,
    A thriving tree to grow.

    Its green and spreading branches
    May flourish, high and fair,
Till comes the bird of Paradise
    To plume her bosom there.
The little Ethiop's mind, beneath
    Its shadow fresh and free,
The wreath may twine — the balm may
        breathe
    Of Immortality !

    Though on the distant waters —
    That others may be fed, —

Of Niger, Nile, or Senegal,
  In faith we cast our bread ;
As rivers from their sources flow,
  Increasing as they roll,
'Twill spring and spread with power, and
      grow,
  To stay the famished soul !

  Whilst here we ply the needle,
    That heathen lands may win
The seamless garment Christ hath wrought,
    To clothe the spirit in ;
Whoe'er but gives a widow's mite,
    Or breathes a Christian prayer,
Will speed our happy angel's flight
    To waft our offering there.

THE LITTLE GLEANER.

Whilst here we're busy gleaning —
  The little birds and I, —
The heavy sheaves are leaning
  Together, bright and dry.
The word that God hath spoken
  In favor of the poor,

So kindly, can't be broken ;
   It is forever sure !

'Tis he who hath commanded
   The reaper of the grain,
When going oft full-handed,
   To let some ears remain.*
By this our Heavenly Father,
   Reveals it, as his will,
That we some bread may gather,
   Who have no fields to till.

The little birds and mother
   And I are poor indeed !
And I've an infant brother
   For her to tend and feed.
So I, their little Lizzie,
   Do all that in me lies,
By keeping ever busy,
   To furnish their supplies.

My father, gone to Heaven,
   Our wants he does not know :
And leave to me is given
   To glean the fields below.

*See Leviticus, xix. 9.

And want will ne'er destroy us,
  While these young hands can toil ;
And mother talk so joyous
  About the *widow's oil !*

The *widow* that we read of,
  Who baked the " little cake "
From meal herself had need of,
  For good Elijah's sake !
She could not send, without it,
  The stranger off distressed —
But you know all about it ;
  How God her barrel blessed !

When all alone I'm gleaning,
  I fancy I can *feel*
And understand the meaning
  Of that increase of meal.
Our God will ne'er forsake us
  Till we forsake his way !
And here's enough to make us
  Our *little cake* to-day.

THE CHILD AND THE HONEY BEE.

Come here, little bee !
There are sweet flowers by me ;

C

Come, and just let me see
How your honey is made.
" Oh! I can't; for I fear
That, for coming too near
I should pay very dear ;
I'm afraid!   I'm afraid!"

O, feel no alarm!
Not a wing nor an arm —
Not a part will I harm,
While you're sipping your fill.
" Pretty maid, then I'll come
Close beside you, and hum ;
And you shall have some
Of the sweets I distil."

My trust then is free,
Just as yours is to me ;
But, be sure, little bee,
Not to give me your sting !
" Oh, no, no ! since I flew
From the cell where I grew,
None has known me to do
So ungrateful a thing !"

Then, why thus supplied
With a sting, but to hide
And to keep never tried,
　　Out of sight? cunning bee!
" He who gave me the sting,
And the swift gauzy wing,
Bids me not harm a thing
　　That would not injure me."

THE MEADOW VIOLET.

Violet, violet, sparkling with dew!
Down in the meadow-land wild where you
　　grew,
How did you come by the beautiful blue
　　In which your soft petals unfold ?
And how do you hold up your tender young
　　head,
When rude sweeping winds rush along o'er
　　your bed,
Or dark, gloomy clouds, ranging over you,
　　shed
　　Their waters, all heavy and cold ?

For no one has nursed you or watched you
    an hour,
Or found you a place in the garden or
    bower;
But art cannot yield me so lovely a flower
   As here I have found at my feet!
O, speak, my sweet violet! answer, and tell
How thus you've grown up, and flourished
    so well,
And live so contented, where lowly you
    dwell,
   And we now by accident meet!

"The same careful hand," the meek violet
    said,
"That holds up the firmament, holds up my
    head!
And He who with azure the skies overspread,
   Has painted the violet blue.
He sprinkles the stars out, above me by
   .   night;
And sends down the sunbeams at morning,
    with light
To make my new coronet sparkling and
    bright,
   When formed of a drop of his dew.

THE GARLAND OF EVERLASTINGS.

"And I've naught to fear from the dark
    heavy cloud,
Or breath of the tempest, that comes strong
    and loud,
Where, born in the lowland, remote from
    the crowd,
    I know and I live but for ONE.
He soon forms a mantle about me to cast,
Of long silken grass, till the rain and the
    blast,
And all that seemed threatening have harm-
    lessly past,
    And clouds scud before the warm sun!"

THE ROSE TREE.

Rose-tree, O my beauteous rose-tree!
    Often have I longed to know
How thy tender leaves were moulded—
    How thy buds are burst, and blow.

I have watered, sunned, and trained thee,
    And have watched thee many an hour;

Yet I never could discover
  How a bud becomes a flower.

So, last night, I thought about thee
  On my pillow, till at last
I was gone in quiet slumber,
  And a dream before me passed.

In it, I beheld my rose-tree
  Stripped of flower, and bud and leaf,
While thy naked stalk and branches
  Filled me with surprise and grief.

Then, methought, I wept to see thee
  Spoiled of all that made thee dear,
Till a band of smiling angels
  Mildly shining, hovered near.

Gently as they gathered round thee
  All in silence, one of them
Laid his fair, soft fingers on thee,
  Pulling leaves from out the stem.

One by one thy twigs he furnished
  With a dress of foliage green;

While another angel followed,
  Bringing buds the leaves between.

Then came one the buds to open ; —
  He their silken rolls unsheathed,
Whilst the one who tints the roses
  Through their opening foldings breathed.

Then the angel of the odors
  Filled each golden-bottomed cell,
Till, between the parting petals,
  Free on air the fragrance fell.

Lifting then their shining pinions,
  Quick the angels passed from sight,
Leaving, where aloft they vanished,
  But a stream of fading light.

There I heard sweet strains of music,
  And their voices far above,
Dying in the azure distance,
  Naming thee *a Gift of Love !*

And my rose-tree stood before me,
  Finished thus by angel hands ; —

Perfect in its bloom and fragrance —
Beautiful, as now it stands!

Hence, whenever I behold thee,
I shall think of angels too;
And the countless works of goodness
They descend on earth to do.

All unseen and silent, round us,
Careful they their watches keep,
Whether we may wake, or slumber;
Guardian angels never sleep!

CHILDREN PRAYING.

Little children, when you pray,
"Father, hallowed be thy name!"
Do you think, the words you say
From the lips of Jesus came?
Uttered not with soul sincere,
They offend his holy ear;
But, if from the heart they rise,
They're as incense to the skies.

When you pray, " Thy kingdom come!"
Would you have it *every where ?*
If you do but think of home,
'Tis a vain and empty prayer.
When you ask " Thy will be done ;"
Every where beneath the sun !
Should a voice within you say,
Or your lips be mute, that pray.

When you ask for " daily bread,"
And your " trespasses " forgiven,
Would you have all people fed ;
Every soul made heir of heaven ?
Then, you 'll strive his name to spread,
Who of life can give the bread ;
Only through whose love can be
Souls from sin, for Heaven made free.

Would you all " temptation " shun,
And " from evil " find release,
Trust to God's beloved son ;
For in him is perfect peace.
What you do his cause to aid,
Will your treasure sure be made,
Where in brightness it shall last
When this earth itself is past !

THE SPIDER.

One biting winter morning,
  A dusky spider swung
From off the mantle, by his thread,
  And o'er the stove-pipe hung.
Escaped from some dim cranny cold,
  To warmer quarters there,
He seemed, upon that slender hold,
  An atom hung on air.

I watched his quick manœuvres
  Above the funnel hot,
Where like a falling mustard seed
  He looked, but touched it not.
For when he'd spun his line too long,
  His tiny hands and feet
He plied to shun the fervor strong,
  And made a slight retreat.

Then down again he'd venture,
  A rash, unwary thing!
And to his tenure frail, above
  The burning iron, cling.
He'd mimic now, the sailor's art
  To dangle on the rope,

And then, the clinging human heart
On some delusive hope.

Methought, " Poor, simple spider !
A cruel death is near ;
Thou art upon its very lip,
And yet so void of fear !
The spider folk, I here confess,
Had never charms for me ;
They weave their tents, like wickedness,
For deeds of cruelty.

" They live by snare and slaughter ;
And oft the piercing cry
I've heard from some poor victim bound,
By them slung up to die ;
The while, for many a venomed bite,
Would spider at him run,
And back, as if with fell delight,
To pain the dying one.

" And yet, I'll try to save thee ; —
For *once* a spider's friend ! "
I raised my hand, when lo ! he fell,
As lightning, to his end !

The wicked flee when none pursue.
  In jealousy and dread,
Not knowing what I aimed to do,
  To death the spider fled.

His little life was over ;
  And where so quick he fell,
Upon the fervid iron lay
  No speck, his fate to tell.
Though short its space, for good or ill,
  We thence, perhaps, may find
Some little moral to distil,
  For use of human kind.

Is not unwary childhood,
  For pleasure, ofttimes prone
To shun the way experience points,
  And bent to take its own ?
Does not the wicked, from his breast,
  Spin out the line of sin
That leads him to the grave unblest,
  And drops him, hopeless, in ?

THE DEWY FLOWER.

The dewy flower that morn unfolds,
  With pure and grateful eye,
Its native earth around beholds,
  Above, the shining sky.

Its pearly crown — a tribute meet —
  To dust beneath it gives ;
And from its heart the odors sweet,
  To Him by whom it lives.

Its spicy breath ascends on air,
  Like childhood's hymn of praise ;
Or seeks its Maker, like the prayer,
  Some infant heart may raise.

Adoring God, delighting man,
  It seems with aim sincere
To serve as far as floweret can
  Its being's purpose here.

Would children emulate the flowers —
  With hearts to God as true,
Would they to him devote their powers,
  What good each child might do !

For God beholds our humblest aim
 To serve his righteous laws ;
To glorify the Savior's name,
 His kingdom and his cause.

Where mind is but a wilderness,
 With souls in heathen night,
Our feeblest efforts he will bless
 To shed the Gospel light.

Some little self-denying deed,
 For heathen land, may shine,
A kindling star ; or like a seed,
 Spring up a fruitful vine.

An owner may come out, and pluck
 His flower, at opening day ;
Or canker at its vitals suck
 Its new-found life away.

And childhood is the morning hour
 Of life's just opening bloom,
When death may snap the dewy flower,
 And lay it in the tomb.

But if at life's bright rising sun
  The heart to God be given,
Though plucked from earth a budded one,
  The soul unfolds in Heaven.

FALSEHOOD FORBIDDEN.

I must not tell a lie,
  Whate'er 's the price to win ;
For God, with his all-seeing eye,
  Would frown upon the sin.

I must not use deceit,
  By any art or wile,
Another's faith and trust to cheat ;
  For God abhors the guile.

They who can falsely smile
  With lips that utter prayer,
Insult their Maker ; and the while
  Are in the tempter's snare.

I must not boldly seek
  My conscience to suppress ;

For soon or late will conscience speak,
And truth obtain redress.

For God enthroned on high,
  Doth out from Heaven declare,
That naught which maketh here a lie,
  Shall find an entrance there.

MARY DOW.

" Come in, little stranger," I said,
  As she tapped at my half-open door,
While the blanket pinned over her head
  Just reached to the basket she bore.

A look full of innocence fell
  From her modest and pretty blue eye,
As she said, " I have matches to sell,
  And hope you are willing to buy.

" A penny a bunch, is the price ;
  I think you 'll not find it too much ;
They're tied up so even and nice,
  And ready to light with a touch."

I asked, " What's your name, little girl ? "
" 'Tis Mary," said she; " Mary Dow."
And carelessly tossed off a curl
That played o'er her delicate brow.

" My father was lost in the deep ;
The ship never got to the shore ;
And mother is sad, and will weep
When she hears the wind blow and sea
roar.

" She sits there, at home, without food,
Beside our poor sick Willie's bed ;
She paid all her money for wood,
And so I sell matches for bread.

" For every time that she tries
Some things she'd be paid for to make,
And lays down the baby, it cries,
And that makes my sick brother wake.

" I'd go to the yard and get chips ;
But then it would make me so sad,
To see men there, building the ships,
And think they had made one so bad.

D

"I've one other gown, and, with care,
 We think it may decently pass,
With my bonnet, that's put by, to wear
 To meeting and sunday school class.

"I love to go there, where I'm taught
 Of one who's so wise and so good,
He knows every action and thought,
 And gives e'en the raven its food.

"For He, I am sure, who can take
 Such fatherly care of a bird,
Will never forget or forsake
 The children who trust to his word.

"And now, if I only can sell
 The matches I brought out to-day,
I think I shall do very well;
 And mother 'll rejoice at the pay."

"Fly home, little bird," then I thought;
 "Fly home full of joy to your nest!"
For I took all the matches she brought,
 And Mary may tell you the rest.

MARY.

Mary, precious is thy name
More than any other
Borne by mortal ; for it came
From our Savior's mother !
Mary pillowed on her breast
Jesus, once, in infant rest :
Now her name, in sacred lines
Traced by inspiration, shines.

Then, another Mary sought
Her beloved Master,
Where he "sat at meat ; " and brought,
Sealed in alabaster,
Costly ointment for his head ;
Brake the box, and o'er him shed
Precious odors, like a cloud
Rising, while to him she bowed.

Still on earth she ever lives,
Young in sacred story ;
Whilst on high to Christ she gives
Endless praise and glory.
Here she "sat at Jesus' feet,"
Listening to his precepts sweet ;

Now she stands with hosts above,
Singing his redeeming love.

Near the cross, when Jesus bled,
    Stood the Marys, weeping ;
Earliest to his tomb they sped,
    Where they thought him sleeping.
When he left his couch of stone,
He to *Mary* first was shown ;
" MARY " was the primal word
From the risen Savior heard.

While arose that Sabbath sun
    Robed in new-made splendor,
Mary was his chosen one,
    First account to render—
First his sorrowing friends to tell
Of the Light of Israel
Showing Death's domain destroyed,
And the grave a final void !

Mary mine, so young and fair,
    Full of warm affection,

Hence from sin and worldly snare
    Wouldst thou sure protection ?
Guard the beauty of thy name
By their graces whence it came :
Early taught of Jesus be,
Like the maid of Bethany.

Choose, like her, " that better part ; "
    Let thine action show it !
If to Christ we give our heart,
    Earth, like Heaven, must know it.
He hath many lovely ways,
Through the child, to perfect praise :
Thou, at least, canst speak and pray
For the heathens far away.

He will bless thy feeblest aim —
    Like that other Mary —
Life to publish in his name,
    Though the means may vary.
Little self-denials, made
Offerings at his altar laid,
On some heathen isle or shore,
May reward thee evermore.

THE FRUIT-TREE BLOSSOM.

My flower, thou art as sweet to me,
　　Thy form as full and fair —
As rich a fruit shall follow thee
As if thou had'st denied the bee
The pure and precious gift that he
　　Wafts joyous through the air.

The spices from thy bosom flow
　　As purely round thee now,
As if withheld an hour ago ;
Restoring, thou canst still bestow ;
Though, whence thy gifts, thou may'st
　　　　not know,
　　Or giving, tell me *how.*

And future good, we yet shall find,
　　Was hidden in thy heart.
Its witness will be left behind,
When thou, like all thy tender kind,
Thy minutes summed, shalt be resigned
　　Forever to depart.

Thy ruin I would not forestall ;
　　Yet soon, I know, to thee

Must come what happens once to all : —
Thy life will fail ; and thou must fall —
Must fade, and perish, past recall
    To vanish from the tree!

Then, on the bough where thou wast sent
    To pass thy fleeting days,
At work for which thine hours were lent,
In silent, balmy, mild content,
A rich and shining monument
    To thee will nature raise!

Now, not in pride — in purpose high,
    Awhile in beauty shine ;
And speak through man's admiring eye,
Forbidding every passer by
To wish to live, or dare to die,
    With object less than thine!

THE BIRD'S HYMN.

My Maker, I know not the place of thy
    home,
If 'tis earth, or the sky, or the sea ;

I only can tell that wherever I roam,
　I've still a kind Father in thee.

I feel that at night when I go to my rest,
　Thy wings all around me are flung ;
And peaceful I sleep, while the down of thy
　　breast
　Is o'er me, as mine o'er my young.

And when in the morning I open my eye,
　I feel thou hast long been awake ;
Thy beautiful plumage is spread o'er the
　　sky,
　And painted on river and lake.

Thy breath has gone into the buds, and the
　　flowers
Have opened to thee on their stems ;
And thou hast strown dew-drops on mea-
　　dows and bowers,
　To glitter like thousands of gems.

Thy voice, in the notes that can only be
　　thine, —
　A music 'tis gladness to hear —

Comes through the green boughs of the
  oak and the pine,
And falls sweet and soft on my ear.

And oft as a shield hast thou stood between
  me
And the arrow that aimed at my heart;
For, though in a form that my eye could
  not see,
I know thou hast parried the dart.

I drink from the drops on the grass and the
  vine,
And gratefully gather my food:
I feel thou hast plenty for me and for mine;
That all things declare thou art good.

My Father, thy pinions are ever unfurled,
  With brightness no changes can dim!
My Maker, thy home is all over the world;
Thou 'lt hear, then, thy bird's lowly hymn.

THE BIRD SET FREE.

She opened the cage, and away there flew
A bright little bird, as a short adieu
It hastily whistled, and passed the door ;
And felt that its sorrowful hours were o'er.

An anthem of freedom it seemed to sing ;
To utter its joy for an outspread wing —
That now it could sport in the boundless air ;
And might go any and every where.

And Anna rejoiced in her bird's delight ;
But her eye was wet, as she marked its flight ;
Till, this was the song that she seemed to
    hear ;
And, merrily warbled, it dried the tear : —

"I had a mistress, and she was kind
In all but keeping her bird confined.
She ministered food and drink to me ;
But oh ! I was pining for liberty !

"My fluttering bosom she loved to smoothe ;
But the heart within it she could not soothe :

I sickened and longed for the wildwood
    breeze,
My feathery kindred, and fresh green trees.

" A prisoner here, with a useless wing,
I looked with sorrow on every thing.
I lost my voice, I forgot my song,
And mourned in silence the whole day long.

" But I will go back with a mellower pipe,
And sing, when the cherries are round and
    ripe ;
On the topmost bough as I lock my feet
To help myself, in my leafy seat.

" My merriest notes shall there be heard
To draw her eye to her franchised bird ;
The burden, then, of my song shall be,
Earth for the wingless ; but air for me ! "

THE LITTLE MAID OF ISRAEL.

A SCRIPTURE STORY.

Ye joyous little maidens
  Of happy Christian land,

Who have the Bible, and are taught
 To read and understand,
A lovely tale those Scriptures tell
 Of one we only know
As *little maid of Israel*,
 She lived so long ago.

For she, so young and nameless,
 A glorious work achieved!
'Twas through her faith, the Syrian lord
 In Israel's God believed.
While she 'mid Syria's idols strove
 To make Jehovah known,
He marked for her a crown above,
 And sealed her here his own.

To Syria borne a captive,
 In Naaman's house a slave,
A missionary sweet she proved,
 Her foreign lord to save.
That honored favorite of the king,
 His chief in rank and power,
Felt on himself an evil cling,
 Corroding every hour.

For Naaman was a leper,
  Whilst all the power and skill
Of magic, art, and pagan rite
  Had failed to reach the ill.
Though clothed in jeweled raiment
    bright
  And golden-wrought array,
His form with leprosy was white,
  To foul disease a prey.

'Twas then this little maiden,
  While serving Naaman's wife,
Was made the means his soul to save,
  And heal his blighted life.
For with that truly pious zeal
  The faithful only know,
She sought his malady to heal, —
  The healing balm to show.

She said, " Would God my master
  Were in Samaria, where
There dwells a Prophet, who would find
  The cleansing secret there! "
But little did the leper know
  How fresh and free and pure

The balsam of the Lord would flow
    His malady to cure.

And Naaman sought Elisha,
    With gifts and rich array ;
When from them all that man of God
    With loathing turned away.
The gift of God he " did not *buy*,
    Nor speak his will for *hire !* "
Then lightning flashed through Naa-
        man's eye
    From out his breast of ire.

The Syrian thought the Prophet
    Would come with grand display ;
And call upon his God with pomp,
    And sacrifice to pay.
But when he merely bade him go,
    And wash in Jordan's tide ;
He deemed it mockery ; spoken so,
    His misery to deride !

" Hath not," he said, " Damascus,
    The city where I dwell,
The better waters, far, than all
    The streams of Israel ?

Abana, there, and Pharpar flow,
In shining fulness seen !
Have they not floods, where I may go
To wash me, and be clean ? "

And had not Naaman's servants
Their master's wrath assuaged,
The leper thence had hastened home,
Despairing and enraged.
As yet the pagan never knew,
'Mid all his keen distress,
What one small act of faith may do,
With Israel's God to bless.

But by his sufferings humbled,
Not knowing where to lean,
He turned and washed him seven times
In Jordan, and was clean !
Renewed in faith, in person fair,
This witness thence he gave :
" No god in all the earth is there,
But Israel's God, to save ! "

Yet of this lovely captive,
The maid of Israel,

And of the mission she performed,
  My song can feebly tell.
You 'll find the tale, and best derive
  The lesson sweet it brings,
By studying it, in chapter five,
  Of Second Book of Kings.

THE SORROWFUL YELLOW-BIRD.

They've caught my little brother;
  And he was to me a twin!
They stole him from our mother;
  And the cage has shut him in.

I flitted by and found him,
  Where he looked so sad and sick,
With the gloomy wires around him,
  As he crouched upon a stick.

And when I tried to cheer him
  With the cherry in my bill,
To see me there so near him —
  Oh! it made him sadder still.

His tender eye was shining
   With the brightness of despair,
With sorrow and repining,
   As he bade me have a care !

He said they'd come and take me,
   As they'd taken him ; and then
A hopeless prisoner make me,
   In the fearful hands of men : —

That, once in their dominion,
   I should have to pine away,
And never stretch a pinion,
   To my very dying day : —

That the wings which God had made
      him
   For freedom in the air,
Since man had thus betrayed him,
   Were stiff and useless there.

And the little darling fellow,
   As he showed his golden breast,
He said, beneath the yellow,
   He'd a sad and aching breast : —

E

That since he'd been among them,
  They had ruffled it so much,
The only song he'd sung them
  Was a shriek beneath their touch.

How can they love to see him
  So sickly and so sad,
When, if they would but free him,
  He'd be so well and glad ?

My hapless little brother !
  I would fain his bondage share :
I never had another ; —
  And he's a captive there !

THE LITTLE FLOWER GARDEN.

In yon old village burying-place,
  With briers and weeds o'ergrown,
I saw a child with beauteous face
  Sit musing all alone.

Without a shoe — without a hat,
  Beside a new-raised mound ;

The little Willie pensive sat,
As if to guard the ground.

I asked him why he lingered thus,
Within that gray old wall.
"Because," said he, "it is to us,
The dearest place of all."

"And what," I asked, "to one so young,
Can make the place so dear ? "
"Our mother"—said the lisping tongue,
"They laid our mother here.

"And since they made it mother's lot,
We like to call it ours : —
We took it for our garden spot,
And planted it with flowers.

"We know 'twas here that she was laid ;
And yet, they tell us, too,
She's now a happy angel, made
To live where angels do.

"Then, will she watch us from above,
And smile on us, to know

That here her little children love
To make sweet flowerets grow.

" My sister Anna's gone to take
Her supper ; and will come,
With quickest haste that she can make,
To let me run for some.

" We do not leave the spot alone,
For fear the birds will spy
The places where the seeds are sown,
And catch them up, and fly !

" We love to have them come, and feed,
And flit and sing about ;
Yet, not where we have dropped the seed,
To find and pick it out.

" But now, the great, round, yellow sun
Is going down the west ;
And soon the birds will, every one,
Be home, and in the nest.

" Then we to rest shall go home too ;
And while we're fast asleep ;

Amid the darkness and the dew,
Perhaps the sprouts will peep!

"And when our plants have grown so high
That leaves are on the stem,
We'll call the pretty birdies nigh,
And scatter crumbs for them.

"For mother loved their songs to hear —
To watch them on the wing;
She'll love to know they still come near
Her little ones, and sing.

"I don't know where's her dwelling-place;
But here, she daily seems
To meet me, as, with smiling face,
She kissed me in my dreams.

"May not she be the Angel, sent
A daily watch to keep;
And, fondly o'er our pillows bent,
To guard us while we sleep?"

"Heaven guard thee, precious child, me-
　　thought,
　"And 'sister Anna,' too ;
And may your future days be fraught
　　With blessings ever new !"

THE LOST HYACINTH.

My hyacinth, my hyacinth
　　At length has come to light !
And round the stalk and purple buds
　　The leaves are green and bright.
Renewed in beauty, it has broke
　　From out the crumbling earth ;
And when I thought it dead and gone,
　　It has another birth !

My hyacinth, my hyacinth,
　　At last I've found thee out !
O, where hast thou been hid so long ?
　　What hast thou been about ?
"I've been," the little hermit said,
　　"Within my lowly cell ;

And joy I've had in quiet there,
That tongue can never tell.

" In sweet communion with the power
To which alone I trust,
I've worshipped long at nature's shrine,
Abased below the dust.
This upper world I find a scene
Of peril, change and strife ;
And from seclusion I must draw
My sweetest draught of life.

" I could not live, if ever thus,
Uncovered to the glare
Of yonder sun, and rudely brushed
By every vagrant air.
'Tis best for me, and best for thee,
That I should pass from sight,
To dwell a while in loneliness,
And hidden from the light.

" For I should lose my highest worth
By being always here ;
And thou would'st lose the joy thou hast
To see me re-appear.

From calm and humble solitude,
  My first attractions flow ;
And but for these, I should be poor,
  Without a charm to show.

"I've now come back to stand awhile
  In beauty to thine eye ;
And when my flowers have gladdened
    thee,
  They 'll be content to die.
And while thy hyacinth shall pour
  Her sweets from every bell,
Remember, she her fragrance gained
  Within the lonely cell!"

THE WINTER KING.*

O! what will become of thee, poor little
  bird ?
The muttering storm in the distance is
  heard ;
The cold winds are waking, the clouds
  growing black !

* *Parus Atricapillus*, Linn. Black-capt Titmouse, Wilson.

They 'll soon scatter snow-flakes all over
    thy back !
From what sunny clime hast thou wandered
    away ?
And what art thou doing, this cold winter
    day ?

" I'm pecking the gum from the old peach-
    tree :
The storm does'nt trouble me ! —Pee-dee-
    dee."

But what makes thee seem so unconscious of
    care ?
The brown earth is frozen — the branches
    are bare !
And how can'st thou seem so light-hearted
    and free,
Like Liberty's form with the spirit of glee,
When no place is near for thine evening
    rest —
No leaf for thy screen — for thy bosom no
    nest ?

"Because the same hand is a shelter for me,
That took off the summer leaves!—Pee-dee-
    dee."

But man feels a burden of want, and of
    grief,
While plucking the cluster and binding the
    sheaf!
We take from the ocean, the earth, and the
    air;
And all their rich gifts do not silence our
    care.
In summer we faint; in the winter we're
    chilled,
With ever a void that is yet to be filled.

"A very small portion sufficient will be,
If sweetened with gratitude!—Pee-dee-dee."

I thank thee, bright monitor! What thou
    hast taught
Will oft be the theme of the happiest
    thought.
We look at the clouds, while the bird has
    an eye

To Him who reigns over them, changeless
    and high !
And now, little hero, just tell me thy name,
That I may be sure whence my oracle came.

"Because, in all weather, I'm happy and
    free,
They call me the ' WINTER KING : ' — Pee-dee-
    dee."

But soon there 'll be ice weighing down the
    light bough
Whereon thou art flitting so merrily now !
And though there's a vesture, well-fitted and
    warm,
Protecting the rest of thy delicate form,
What then wilt thou do with thy little bare
    feet,
To save them from pain, 'mid the frost and
    the sleet ?

"I can draw them right up in my feathers,
    you see !
To warm them, and fly away ! — Pee-dee-
    dee."

THE BOY AND THE FLOWERS.

Radiant with his spirit light,
  Was the happy little child,
Sporting round a fountain bright,
  Playing through the flowerets wild.
Where they grew he lightly stepped,
  Cautious not a leaf to crush ;
Then about the fount he leaped,
  Shouting at its merry gush.

While the sparkling waters welled,
  Laughing as they bubbled up,
In his lily hand he held,
  Closely clasped, a silver cup.
Now he put it forth to fill ;
  Then he bore it to the flowers,
Through his fingers there to spill
  What it held, in mimic showers.

" Open, pretty buds," said he,
  " Open to the air and sun ;
So to-morrow I may see
  What my rain to-day has done.
Yes, you will, you will, I know,
  For the drink I give you now,

Burst your little cups, and blow,
   When I'm gone, and can't tell how.

" Oh! I wish I could but see
   How God's finger touches you,
When your sides unclasp, and free,
   Let the spice and petals through.
I would watch you all the night;
   Nor in darkness be afraid,
Only once to see aright
   How a beauteous flower is made.

"Now remember, I shall come
   In the morning, from my bed,
Here to find among you, some
   With your brightest colors spread!"
To his buds he hastened out
   At the dewy morning hour,
Crying with a joyous shout,
   " God has made of each a flower!"

Precious must the ready faith
   Of the little children be,
In the sight of Him who saith,
   " Suffer them to come to me."

Answered by the smile of Heaven
Is the infant's offering found,
Though " a cup of water given,"
Even to the thirsty ground!

ROBIN, SING TO ME.

Robin, robin, sing to me,
And I'll gladly suffer thee
Thus to breakfast in the tree,
    On the ruddy cherry.
Soon as thou hast swallowed it,
How I love to see thee flit
To another twig, and sit,
    Singing there, so merry.

It was kind in thee to fly
Near my window ; and to try
There to raise thy notes so high
    As to break my slumbers.
Robin, half the cheering power
Of this bright and lovely hour,
While I pluck the dewy flower,
    Comes from thy sweet numbers !

And thou wast an honest bird,
Thus to let thy voice be heard,
Asking — in the plainest word
 Thou could'st utter — whether
Those who owned it, would allow
Thee to take upon the bough
Thy repast, and sit, as now,
 Smoothing down thy feather.

Who, that hears the mellow note
On the air of morning float
From the robin's little throat,
 Could desire to still her?
Who her beauty can behold,
And consent to have it told,
That he had a heart so cold,
 As to try to kill her?

THE CHILDREN AT THE OAK.

Beneath an old oak's leafy shade,
  In careless infant glee,
Three little children sat, and played,
  Or chased about the tree.

So light and airily they went,
  With each a beaming face,
The grass beneath their footsteps bent,
  Sprang back, and took its place.

The flowers they'd plucked and carried
      there,
  Lay scattered all around,
And spread their odors on the air,
  While they adorned the ground.

A bright embroidery they made,
  To decorate the scene,
In sweet confusion, lightly laid
  Upon the silken green.

As round the tree they ran and leapt,
  Those gladsome little boys
Upon the last year's acorns stepped,
  And gathered them for toys.

When down they sat, to count them o'er,
  Beneath those branches high,
That once the pretty play-things bore,
  An aged man drew nigh.

His hair was white—his eye was dim;
  So slow his way he made,
The children, rising, ran to him,
  And led him to the shade.

When, braced against the firm old oak,
  And leaning on his staff,
He listened, while the prattlers spoke,
  And joined their childish laugh.

F

Then every acorn offered up,
  With smooth and pointed cone
Set close within its bossy cup,
  Was to the patriarch shown.

Said he, " My little children dear,
  Take each an acorn sound,
And, though an old man's word you hear,
  Go hide it in the ground.

" For every one a future oak
  Contains within its shell ;
And when the germ its sheath has broke,
  'Twill peer from out the cell.

" Then three young trees, all firm and
      bright,—
  And *this* — in swift decay,
Will stand in their beholder's sight,
  As we, in ours, to-day.

" My father, when a playful child
  But in his seventh year,
An acorn from the forest wild
  Brought out, and planted here.

"Thence rose the good old tree, which thus
    Throws wide its leafy veil,
And stands, while overshadowing us,
    A witness to my tale.

"And even to his latest days,
    By planting seed or shoot,
He loved the infant tree to raise
    For future shade or fruit.

"For while he knew he might not see
    The blossom deck the limb,
He reared them as a good to be
    For others after him.

"When, feeling life's swift years were spent,
    He saw its end appear,
He asked to have his monument
    The oak he planted here.

"And now, beneath this grassy mound
    In nature's beauty dressed,
Which you have scattered flowers around,
    His hallowed ashes rest.

" And I, in every blooming year
    From infancy till now,
Have listened to the warblers here,
    That sang from bough to bough.

" Full fourscore summers have I come
    To hear their carol gay ;
And yet they seem but as the sum
    Of hours that make a day !

" While hence I've viewed the plant and
        flower
    That decked the hill and mead,
They seemed epistles, traced by Power
    Above, for man to read.

" When o'er my head, soft winds passed by,
    And threw the leaves apart,
Methought sweet whispers from the sky,
    Were breathed upon my heart.

" They seemed my father's angel voice,
    In tones of peace and love,
That bade me make my early choice
    A treasure pure above.

ROSA AND AGNES.

"For he, when, but a child, he laid
  In earth the acorn low,
Resigned his heart to Him who made
  The oak spring up, and grow.

"That God, who called my father hence
  From sorrow, pain, and dust,
Was then his orphan's sure defence, —
  Is now my joy and trust.

"'Tis he who makes the old man smile,
  Though trembling, hoar, and dim;
For now 'tis but a little while
  Ere I shall be with Him!"

The speaker ceased; when, quick and
    mute,
  Each listener stepped apart;
In earth to lay the oaken fruit,
  As faith lay in his heart

THE SPARROW.

A quiet, harmless little bird,
  About your door I come ;
And when my low " chick-chick," is heard,
  I'm asking for a crumb.
O'er mint and clover-tops I flit,
  And through the fragrant yarrow ;
Then, waiting near your door I sit,
  A patient little sparrow.

To yon old churchyard late I flew,
  And from its gate looked round,
Where marble stood, and willows grew,
  Within the silent ground.
The branches drooped, the graven stone
  Gazed on the grassy barrow ;
But all was hush, and there was none
  Awake to hear the sparrow.

In simple suit of russet brown,
  I thus am daily dressed,
While other birds on me look down ;
  Yet I've a peaceful breast.

No envy for the loud and gay
  Shall e'er my bosom harrow ;
More lowly, I'm more blest than they,
  A fearless, trustful sparrow !

For clearer note, and richer plume,
  And wider wings to fly,
May others higher rank assume
  On nature's scale, than I.
Yet crimson, azure, green and gold
  Attract the archer's arrow :
Bright captives, too, the *cage* may hold,
  That never held a sparrow !

Now, lady, lest around your door
  The bird that comes to-day
A crumb to ask, may come no more,
  At heart my message lay.
For I'm our Maker's *carrier-bird*,
  Though seems my sphere so narrow ;
And 'tis a kindly Spirit-word
  He sendeth by " the sparrow ! "

THE GOOD DOLL.

Come, sister dear,
I'll read you here
The story of a Dollie,
Who never strayed
Nor disobeyed
Good rules, by guilt or folly.

She never cried,
When put aside,
In bed or in the cradle;
When taken up,
She broke no cup,
Nor dropped a spoon or ladle.

She never told
A fib, nor rolled
Her pretty lip in anger;
Nor, if displeased,
Felt cross, and teased,
Or filled the house with clangor.

She never soiled
Her dress, or spoiled

Her shoes, their worth abusing ;
  Nor did she tear
  Her book, or wear
Through leaves she was perusing.

  She did not pass
  Before the glass
Too often, or too vainly ;
  As if her worth
  Should be set forth
In outward beauty mainly.

  The whole, in short,
  Of Dollie's fort,
Was trust in those to train her
  Who better knew
  Than she could do,
Wherein she'd be a gainer.

  A brother young
  Was found among
Miss Dollie's near relations,
  Who could, like her,
  Some good infer
From slightest intimations.

But both were small ;
So this is all
Their story gives at present :
It lets us see,
How each could be
In aspect always pleasant.

THE ROBIN'S SONG.

Hark ! it is the robin's song
　　Coming through the flowery trees !
Sweetly does it float along
　　Hither, on the balmy breeze.

O, that I could understand
　　Once, the meaning of the words
Warbled forth so quick, to go
　　To the music of the birds !

If I had him in my hand,
　　Holding down his glossy wings,
Could I better understand
　　What it is the robin sings ?

Were his tender downy breast
    Pressing, warm, upon my palm,
Could I make it feel at rest?
    Would he then be tame and calm?

No, — upon his native bough
    He is happy, light and free :
There, to Heaven he carols now
    Praises for his liberty!

Captive, he would only make
    Signs of anguish — sounds of grief,
Till his little heart would break,
    Mourning — panting — for relief.

He who formed the feathered lyre,
    Hath the light, unfettered wings
Made to fan the latent fire
    Kindled in the hidden strings.

Whilst he holds it high in air,
    To his touch it quick replies ;
But if mortal fingers bear
    On its chords, the music dies!

THE CHILD AND THE FIRE-FLY.

Come here, pretty fly,
　　For the grass is so damp
And the wind is so high,
　　They will put out your lamp.

Come, don't be so coy,
　　Flashing by me with fear ;
There's naught to destroy,
　　Or to injure you here.

Like a bright little spark
　　As you're flying about,
Here and there, in the dark,
　　O, you *will* get put out !

Then come, pretty fly,
　　Here's a shelter for you :
Not a blast shall come nigh,
　　Nor a drop of the dew.

Secure shall you stand,
　　Little jewel, and shed
Your light in my hand,
　　When your winglets are spread ;

Or rest here by me,
  In the pure crystal cup ;
If you 'll just let me see
  How your winglets go up.

" Many thanks for your care,"
  Said the wise little fly ;
" But without dew and air,
  I should soon faint and die.

" More charms do I find
  In a fresh blade of grass,
Than appears, to my mind,
  In a whole house of glass !

" My lamp is not made
  Of the poor, wasting oil,
With burning to fade,
  Or for dampness to spoil.

" By a hand that's unseen
  It is fashioned and trimmed ;
And this is the screen
  That shall keep it undimmed.

"Secure in that hand,
    I can live at my ease,
And glow while I'm fanned
    By the blast and the breeze.

"I love to be free,
    And to feel the whole world
Is open to me
    When my wings are unfurled.

"From a sweet verdant sod
    Am I raised up at night,
When the brightness of God
    Lends the Fire-fly her light!"

THE BIRD'S HOME.

O, where is thy home, sweet bird
With the song, and bright glossy plume?
    "I'll tell thee where I rest,
    If thou wilt not rob my nest;
I built among the sweet apple-bloom!"

But, what's in thy nest, bright bird?
What's there, in the snug downy cell?
"If thou wilt not rob the tree;
    Nor go too near, to see
My quiet little home, I will tell."

O, I will not thy trust betray!
The secret I will closely keep.
"I've three tender little things
    That have never used their wings!
I left them there, at home, fast asleep."

Then, why art thou here, my bird,
Away from thy young, helpless brood?
"To pay thee with a song
    Just to let me pass along,
Nor harm me, as I look for their food."

THE BROKEN PIPE.

Come here, little Willie;
    Why, what is the trouble?
"I've broke my new pipe, ma'—
    I can't make a bubble!"

Well, don't weep for that, child ;
  Come brighten your face,
And tell how this grievous
  Disaster took place.

" Why, Puss came along,
  And said I, 'Now she'll think
This white frothy water
  Is milk she may drink.'

" So, I set it before her,
  And plunged her mouth in,
When up came her paws,
  And clung fast to my chin.

" Then I gave her a blow
  With my pipe ; and it flew
At once into pieces !—
  O, what shall I do ?

" I can't make a bubble !
  I wish naughty Kit
Had been a mile off :
  See, there's blood on me yet ! "

I'm sorry, my boy ; though
   Your loss is but just.
You first deceived Pussy,
   And trifled with trust.

And failing in this,
   You compelled her ; and thence
The wound on your face
   From poor Kit's self-defence.

Then when you grew cruel,
   And beat her, you know
Your pipe and yourself
   Fared the worst for the blow.

Let this lesson teach you,
   Hence never to stoop,
To make man or brute,
   That may trust you, a dupe ;

That when you have power,
   It should not be abused,
Oppressing the weaker,
   Nor strength be misused.

G

For often unkindness
　　Returns whence it came ;
Deceit, too, will ever
　　Be followed by shame.

Remember this, William,
　　And here end your sorrow :
I 'll buy you a pipe,
　　To make bubbles, to-morrow.

THE PEACH BLOSSOMS.

Come here! come here, cousin Mary, and see
What fair, ripe peaches there are on the
　　tree —
On the very same bough that was given to
　　me
　　By father, one day last spring.
When it looked so beautiful, all in the blow,
And I wanted to pluck it, he told me, you
　　know,
I might, but that waiting a few months
　　would show
　　The fruit, that patience might bring.

And as I perceived, by the sound of his
    voice,
And the look of his eye, it was clearly his
    choice
That it should not be touched, I have now
    to rejoice
  That I told him we'd let it remain ;
For, had it been gathered when full in the
    flower,
Its blossoms had withered, perhaps, in an
    hour,
And nothing on earth could have given the
    power
  That would make them flourish again.

But now, of a fruit so delicious and sweet
I've enough for myself and my playmates a
    treat ;
And they tell me, besides, that the kernels
    secrete
  What, if planted, will make other trees :
For the shell will come open to let down the
    root ;
A sprout will spring up, whence the branch-
    es will shoot ;

There'll be buds, leaves and blossoms ; and
    then comes the fruit —
Such beautiful peaches as these !

THE BIRD'S MATERNAL CARE.

The following is but versified statement of a touching, literal
fact that occurred not long since a few rods from my own door.

A shadowy tree, that grew beside
    Its city owner's door,
Its branches threw so high and wide,
That many a bird could sing, and hide
    Among the leaves it bore.

A robin came, and built her nest
    In that green rustling tree.
At evening, there she sank to rest
And furled her weary wings, as blest
    As little bird could be.

Upon her side her drowsy head,
    Beneath her folded wing,
She pillowed, while the night-hours fled :

When morning flushed the east with red,
　She'd wake, and mount, and sing.

Five pretty eggs of azure hue,
　In that soft nest she laid.
So clear and vivid was their blue,
Like polished balls they shone to view,
　Of purest sapphire made.

And many a day she brooded o'er
　Those treasures, till they grew,
In what the shells contained before,
To something different — something more —
　Young birds came peeping through !

Five little baby birds were there,
　In that fond robin's nest,
All callow ; and their mother's care
Was now to find their daily fare,
　And shield them with her breast.

Her tiny game, or berries ripe
　From some far distant stem
She'd bring them ; then her beak she'd wipe,
And sit upon a twig, and pipe
　A mother's tune to them.

At length, the owner of the tree
    One dismal, stormy day,
His window from the shade to free,
The better in his room to see,
    Some branches lopped away.

He dropped the very bough that hung
    A curtain o'er the nest.
The sun burnt through the clouds, and flung
His fire the helpless brood among,
    Till they were sore oppressed.

Their tender mother then was seen
    To stand on weary feet,
Where now they missed the leafy green,
With one wing raised her babes to screen
    From sultry noontide heat.

And, patient there, she day by day,
    Upon her nest's round edge,
Stood up to keep the sun away,
While, shaded thus, her nestlings lay
    Till time their forms could fledge.

Then, when the master of the tree
  Beheld what love and care
Within a mother bird could be,
He wished in vain that he could see
  The bough still living there.

Thus, thoughtless we may often pain
  Or grieve a feeling heart,
Wherein the anguish must remain,
While we may wish, but wish in vain,
  To lay or lull the smart.

A good destroyed 's a fearful thing,
  And so 's a good undone!
We, serving self, on self may bring
A heavier ill — a keener sting
  Than what we sought to shun.

'T is little acts of good or ill,
  That make our vast account.
No one, though great, does *all* God's will.
Small drops the caves of ocean fill ;
  And sands compose the mount.

THE WHEAT FIELD.

Field of wheat, so full and fair,
Shining, with thy sunny hair
Lightly waving either way,
Graceful as the breezes play —
Looking like a summer sea, —
How I love to gaze at thee!
Pleasant art thou to the sight;
And to thought, a rich delight.
Then, thy voice is music sweet,
Softly-sighing Field of Wheat.

Pointing to the genial sky,
Rising straight, and aiming high,
Every stalk is seen to shoot
As an arrow, from the root.
Like a well-trained company,
All, in uniform, agree
From the footing to the ear ;
All in order strict appear.
Marshaled by a skilful hand,
All together bow, or stand —
Still, within the proper bound ;
None o'ersteps the given ground —
With its tribute held to pay

At His nod whom they obey.
Each the gems that stud its crown
Will ere long for man lay down :
Thou with promise art replete
Of the precious sheaves of wheat.

How thy strength in weakness lies !
Not a robber-bird that flies
Finds support whereby to put
On a stalk her lawless foot ;
Not a predatory beak
Plunges down, thy stores to seek,
Where the guard of silver spears
Keeps the fruit, and decks the ears.
No vain insect, that could do
Harm to thee, dares venture through
Such an armory, or eat
Off the sheath, to take the wheat.

What a study do we find
Opened here for eye and mind !
In it, who can offer less
Than to wonder, and confess,
That on this high-favored ground,
Faith is blest, and *Hope* is crowned ?

Charity her arms may spread
Wide from it, with gifts of bread.
Wisdom, Power, and Goodness meet
In the bounteous Field of Wheat!

THE WHITE ANEMONE.

Thy charm, pale, modest, timid one,
Is this — that thou dost ever shun
The public walk, and to the sun
  Dost show an open heart;
Which does not fear the brightest ray
That's darted from the eye of day,
Will aught of secret stain betray,
  Or find a double part.

And thou hast never been beguiled
To quit the simple, quiet wild
Where Nature placed her modest child
  To worship her alone.
Thou dost not ask the brow of toil
To shed its costly dew, to spoil
The bed of free, unfurrowed soil
  Which thou hast made thine own.

And now, if I were hence to take
Thee, root and stem, it would but make
Thee homesick — and the spell would
    break,
  That 's round the desert gem.
So, I will set me down, and look
On thy fair leaves, my little book,
To read the name of Him who took
  Such care in forming them.

PIC-NIC HYMN.

When Jesus the multitude fed,
  And blest the repast brought before them,
The earth was the table he spread, —
  The skies, the pavilion hung o'er them.
And He, the great Teacher, is ours!
  From Art and the world thus retiring,
We find, through grass, wild-wood and
    flowers,
  His wisdom and goodness transpiring.

When nature we read in the leaves
  And bloom of the trees, softly spreading,

Our spirit fresh vigor receives,
　　As if walks of Paradise treading.
The insect that chirps at our feet, —
　　The breeze in the branches surrounding, —
The birds, with their songs wildly sweet,
　　Are notes to the Deity sounding.

And we to Him, present alone,
　　Save Nature's sweet angel, confiding
Our soul's deepest feelings, must own
　　No good like his favor abiding!
The streamlet — the floweret — the tree —
　　The mountain majestic and hoary ; —
Yea, all that we hear, or we see,
　　Attests to his power and his glory.

His Book spreads from earth to the skies!
　　The more we its leaves are unfolding,
The more it enlightens our eyes
　　His higher perfections beholding.
Embellished with stars and the sun,
　　It shines ; and for clear *illustration*,
To us the Omnipotent One
　　Hath sent his Divine REVELATION.

THE FLY UNDER THE LAMP-SHADE.

Ah! thou lost, unwary thing,
Fluttering with a tortured wing —
Crying, with thy little feet
Scorched amid surrounding heat!
Poor, unhappy, suffering fly,
What a painful death to die!

Since so rashly thou hast strayed
'Twixt the funnel and the shade,
In the fiery prison lost,
Now thy life must pay the cost
Of thy venturing near the glare
Dazzling to allure thee there!

Oh! it fills my heart with pain
Thus to see thee strive in vain
For escape ; for I, alas!
Am too small to lift the glass.
Mother says I must not take
Things my little hands might break.

Here she comes! but 'tis too late!
Thou, poor thing, hast met thy fate.

Motion ceases — life has fled —
Dropping on the table, dead,
Now I see thee, thoughtless fly,
'Twas a foolish death to die!

"Yes, my child, in careless play,
Thus his life is thrown away.
For a thing that pleased the eye
He rushed onward but to die!
But remember — there was none
Warning him the blaze to shun.

"If thou think'st the untaught flies,
For their errors, so unwise,
Let this insect's fall be hence
From temptation thy defence.
On thy heart a picture stamp
Of *the fly about the lamp!*"

THE BIBLE IN THE FIELDS.

I love to take this holy book,
In summer's balmy hours,

To study it beside the brook,
Or by the trees and flowers.

For here I read about the God
Who made this world so fair,
The skies — the stream — the grassy sod
And bloom, that scents the air.

The birds flit round, and sweetly sing
Of Him, who feeds them all, —
Who lifts the towering eagle's wing,
And marks the sparrow's fall.

The violet, from its soft green bed
To speak his goodness too,
Presents its tender, purple head
Baptized with silvery dew.

And here the busy bee I view,
As she comes swiftly by,
And seems to ask, if she should do
More work, or good than I.

Her waxen house betimes to build
I see her wisely bent ;

And then, with bread and honey filled
To have it, still intent.

The bees I find their sweets supplied
In wild Judea's land,
To feed the Baptist, when he cried,
"Heaven's kingdom is at hand."

And when our Savior, from the grave,
Had asked his friends for meat,
He ate the honey-comb they gave;
And showed his hands and feet.

This volume of his will revealed
I here can read within,
"Behold the lilies of the field —
They neither toil nor spin!"

And yet the king "was not arrayed
In glory, like to them;"
Their Maker's power is so displayed
In flower and leaf and stem.

And he sat on the mountain's side,
Who spake these blessed words,

Before him flowery fields spread wide —
Around were trees and birds.

The fleecy flocks that roam so free
On hill and valley deep,
I love to watch : and here I see
'Tis written, " Feed my sheep."

For thus I seem to keep in view,
And feel how near I am
To that dear Friend of Children who
Has named himself " The LAMB."

WRITING IN HELEN'S ALBUM, ON
HER BIRTH-DAY.

Now, Helen dear, I hear thee say,
That thou art six years old to-day !
So I will set my record here
Of thy beginning seventh year,
That thou in after days may'st find
The trace which this has left behind.

H

This morning we together strayed
'Mid fern, and brake, and forest-shade ;
    And, with thy little hand in mine,
    We passed the rustling oak and pine,
Where last year's acorn-cup and cone
Among its withered leaves were strown.

The nimble squirrel, climbing high,
Looked down on us with curious eye ;
    While birds amid the branches sung
    Till through the woods their music rung;
And in the boughs the spicy breeze
Made leafy air-harps of the trees.

Round, scarlet berries, ripe and sweet,
Peeped out like gems beside our feet ;
    The modest harebell bowed beneath
    The sweetbrier tall, her balm to breathe;
And many a little floweret wild
Grew low, but looked to heaven and
    smiled.

We ventured down the mossy steep,
That edged the waters clear and deep,

Where blooming laurels grew beside
The Merrimack's broad silver tide ;
And all was beauteous, fresh, and fair,
In nature's glory shining there.

And may thy future days be bright —
Thy heart be ever pure and light,
   As when, a little gladsome child,
   I led thee through the flowery wild ;
And by thy prattling tongue was told,
That thou to-day wast six years old !

In other days, when thou may'st see
My face no more, remember me —
   Remember, that I asked to-day
   Heaven's smile upon thy future way —
That 'twas thy parent's early friend,
And thine, who this memento penned.

LADY MARY.

Lady Mary was able
To keep a good table ;

And what was still better, none found her
　　Without a good heart
　　The good things to impart,
Which Providence showered around her.

　　She was prudent, 'tis true;
　　But was generous, too,
When charity called for her money;
　　And she ever kept by,
　　Her own board to supply,
Fresh biscuits, sweet butter and honey;

　　And twenty things more
　　That we'll not number o'er,
But such as gave comfort to many
　　So old, lone and poor,
　　That at home she felt sure,
They had very little, if any.

　　Then, oft as there came
　　To her house some old dame,
So feeble she scarce could walk steady,
　　Lady Mary would say,
　　"Take your cloak off and stay,
And early my tea shall be ready."

So pleasant her smile
And her manners the while —
So kind was the welcome she gave her,
Her modest old guest
Would be put quite at rest,
And stay as if granting a favor.

She'd laugh, then, and chat,
About this thing and that,
And seek to amuse her meek hearer,
As social and free,
While she poured out the tea,
As if some great duchess were near her.

When the moment was come
For her guest to go home,
That she might neither want, beg, nor borrow,
She'd press her to take
A nice tart and a cake,
Or something else, good for the morrow.

She sometimes would go
Soothing words to bestow,
With gifts and kind looks, where were lying

The sick, pale, and faint;
And she'd kneel, like a saint,
In prayer by the bed of the dying.

Her wish was, to see
All as happy as she:
And she knew her kind deeds so to vary,
    That the sad, rich and poor,
    Said, in heaven, they were sure,
Was a place for the good lady Mary.

THE TRAMMELED FLY.

Ah, thou unfortunate!
  Poor silly fly,
Caught in the spider's web —
  Hung there to die!
What could have tempted thee?
  What led thee there,
For the foe thus to throw
  Round thee the snare?

Struggling and crying so
  Ne'er can unweave

From thee the silken threads
    Laid to deceive.
Sorrow for wandering
    Comes now in vain ;
And with one thus undone,
    Grief adds to pain.

Yet I will rescue thee,
    Unwary thing !
Thou may'st again be off
    High on the wing ;
If thou wilt promise me,
    Hence to be found
Never more, as before
    On evil ground.

Trust not the flatterer
    Skilled to ensnare :
He is a wily one ;
    Think, and beware !
Down to his dusky ways
    No more descend.
Little fly, thou and I
    Want each a friend.

Man hath an enemy :
　His snare is laid
Softly and silently,
　Deep in the shade.
Light, by the tempter shunned,
　Only can show
Where, secure, free, and pure,
　Our feet may go!

THE WHITE MOTH.

Beware, pretty Moth, so unsullied and white,
　Beware of the lamp's dazzling rays!
It is not a drop of the sun, but a light
That shines to allure little rovers by night;
　Away! there is death in the blaze.

O, why didst thou come from thy covert of
　　green,
　The vine, round my window so bright;
And pop in to know what was here to be
　　seen,
Forsaking thy shield, and escaping thy
　　screen,
　And hazarding life by the flight?

The down on thy limbs and thy bosom so pure
 That flame would most fatally singe :
And nothing thy beautiful wings can insure
From harm and from pain beyond mending
  or cure,
 If caught by their delicate fringe.

Return, giddy wanderer, safe to the vine ;
 And breathe in the fresh evening air ;
Go, look at the stars, as they twinkle and
  shine ;
And cling to a leaf, or the tendrils that
  twine,
 — My soft little eavesdropper, there !

And then, by a song I will sing, thou shalt
  know,
 Why thus I have lifted my arm
To scare thee away from thy luminous foe,
That threw out its beams, as a snare, and a
  show
 To tempt the unwary to harm.

For, I through the day, have been guarded
 by One,

Who, greater and wiser than I,
Has pitied my frailty ; and forced me to
    shun
Illusive temptations, where I might have run
    The peril of sporting to die.

'Twas kindness from Him, to whose care I
    commend
Myself through the darkness of night,
That taught me so quick to come in, as a
    friend,
Between thee and evil, thy life to defend ;
    Pretty Moth, so unsullied and white.

LITTLE ELLEN, AND HER BROKEN BASKET.

As Ellen — now Ellen's a sweet little girl,
　An infantine, innocent creature ;
With cheeks like the rose-petal, teeth like
　　the pearl,
　· And lovely in every feature ; —

As Ellen one day, all equipped for a walk,
　Went forth with the nurse, from her
　　mother ;
And looked like a bud that was broke from
　　its stalk,
　And lodged, in its fall, on another.

She had not gone far, when she spied on the
　　green,
　A bird, that she thought had just lighted ;
The largest and tamest she ever had seen,
　Which seemed neither jealous nor frighted.

And so, from the hand of the nurse getting
    free,
  She bounded off nearer, to watch it.
"O see what a beautiful creature!" said
    she,
  "I guess little Ellen can catch it."

Then, running, she stepped on her frock-hem,
    and fell,
  Or, as sometimes we say, made a blunder :
The bird raised its wings, with a hideous
    yell,
  Which capping the fall, nearly stunned
    her.

And Ellen, intent upon catching the bird,
  Which she did not yet know by its feather,
Came down on her neat little basket, and
    heard
  Its sides crushed, like egg-shells, together!

The name of the bird may not here be of use,
  Yet some little querist may ask it ;
I therefore will tell you, — 'twas chasing a
    Goose,
That spoiled Ellen's beautiful basket!

TO ADELAIDE,

WHO GAVE ME THE CAPE-JASMINE.

[Written in her Album.]

A Jasmine opening, sweet and fair,
　Was late thy gift to me ;
And naught have I, that can compare
　With this, to offer thee.

But from my poet-spirit's bower,
　Whose paths not foot can trace,
I bring this little dewy flower
　Among thy leaves to place.

And when these earth-born flowers depart,
　As spring and summer fly,
A keepsake, hold it in thy heart,
　So it may never die.

Its petals are perfumed with prayer,
　That God may bless thy ways,
And give his holy angels care
　O'er all thy mortal days.

For life with thee is in its spring ;
　Its landscape fresh and bright ;

While Hope is on her morning wing,
  Nor thinks of coming night!

The things of time would fain possess
  Thy soul beyond release ;
But *Wisdom's ways are pleasantness ;*
  And all her paths are peace !

If now thy heart in youthful glow
  Devote to God its love,
Through shade, and storm, and frost below,
  Thy Star will shine above!

THE SNOW-FLAKE.

" Now, if I fall, will it be my lot
  To be cast in some low and lonely spot,
  To melt, and to sink, unseen or forgot?
    And there will my course be ended ? "
'Twas this a feathery Snow-flake said,
  As down through measureless space it
    strayed ;
Or, half by dalliance, half afraid,
  It seemed in mid air suspended.

"Oh, no!" said the Earth, "thou shalt
    not lie
Neglected and lone, on my lap to die,
Thou pure and delicate child of the sky!
    For thou wilt be safe in my keeping.
But then I must give thee a lovelier form;
Thou wilt not be part of the wintery
    storm;
But revive, when the sunbeams are yellow
    'and warm,
    And the flowers from my bosom are
    peeping!

"And then I will give thee thy choice, to be
Restored in the lily that decks the lea;
In the pure jasmine-bloom, the anemone,
    Or aught of thy spotless whiteness;
To melt, and be cast in a glittering bead,
With the pearls that the night scatters
    over the mead,
In the cup where the bee and the fire-fly
    feed,
    Regaining thy dazzling brightness.

"I'll let thee awake from thy transient
    sleep,

When Viola's mild blue eye shall weep,
In a tremulous tear ; or a diamond, leap
  In a drop from the unlocked fountain ;
Or, leaving the valley, the meadow and
    heath,
The streamlet, the flowers, and all beneath,
Go up, and be wove in a silvery wreath
  Encircling the brow of the mountain.

" Or, would'st thou return to a home in the
    skies,
To shine in the Iris, I 'll let thee arise,
And appear in the many and glorious dyes
  A pencil of sunbeams is blending !
But true, fair thing, as my name is Earth,
I 'll give thee a new and vernal birth,
When thou shalt recover thy primal worth,
  And never regret descending !"

" Then I will drop," said the trusting flake ;
"But bear it in mind, that the choice I
    make
Is not in the flowers, nor the dew to
    awake ;
  Nor the mist, that shall pass with the
    morning.

For, things of thyself, they will die with
    thee ;
But those that are lent from on high, like
    me,
Must rise, and will live, from thy dust set
    · free,
To the regions above returning.

"If true to thy word and just thou art,
Like the spirit that dwells in the holiest
    heart,
Unsullied by thee, thou wilt let me depart,
    And return to my native heaven.
For I would be placed in the beautiful
    Bow,
From time to time in thy sight to glow,
So thou may'st remember the Flake of
    Snow
By the Promise that God hath given ! "

THE WIDOW'S ONLY SON.

She wrapped her in her sable cloak,
    And walked beside the sea ;

I

But seldom of her sorrow spoke,
　So full of grief was she.

'Twas this that made her heart so sad,
　To view the ocean wide : —
The only son that widow had
　Went out to sea and died.

And then in that great rolling deep,
　With solemn, tearful eyes,
His messmates lowered him down, to
　　sleep
　Till all the dead shall rise.

But where, among those waters vast,
　With ceaseless fall and swell,
Her child to that repose had passed,
　The mother could not tell.

She therefore questioned wave on wave,
　That heaving, reached the shore,
If they had rolled across his grave
　Whom she should see no more.

And often when she saw a ship
　With home-returning sail,

Would ashy paleness seize her lip,
And speech and vision fail.

For oh! she thought about the one
That spread its canvas white,
To waft away her only son
Forever from her sight.

But still, amid the bitter grief
That wrung that widow's heart,
Her bosom felt the sweet relief
That faith and hope impart.

She knew her son had ever kept
The path to Heavenly rest;
That when he sunk in death, he slept
Upon a Savior's breast.

" My Heavenly Father," she would say,
" The deep and troubled sea
But holds from me the precious clay;
My child 's at home with thee!"

THE CHILD'S HYMN TO SPRING.

Thou lovely and glorious Spring,
  Descending to us from the sky,
I praise thee for coming to bring
  Such beautiful things to my eye!

For, bearing thine arms full of flowers
  To strew o'er the earth, hast thou come,
Adorning this low world of ours
  With brightness like that of thy home.

And thou hast brought back the gay birds,
  Their songs full of gladness to sing —
To give, in their musical words,
  Their sweet little anthems to Spring!

The roots thou hast watered and fed ;
  The leaves thou hast opened anew ;
The violet lifts its meek head,
  And seems as 'twere praising thee, too.

The hills thou hast made to rejoice,
  And all their young buds to unfold ;
The cowslips spring up at thy voice,
  And dot the green meadows with gold.

The brooks o'er the pebbles that run
  Are sounding thy praise as they go ;
The grass points its blades to the sun,
  And thanks thee for making them grow.

The rush and the delicate reed
  Are waving in honor of thee, —
The lambkins are learning to feed —
  The honey-cup 's filled for the bee.

The butterfly 's out on the wing —
  The spices are out on the breeze ;
And sweet is the breathing of Spring
  That comes thro' the blossoming trees !

The forest, the grove and the vine
  In festival vestures are clad,
To show that a presence like thine
  Is making them grateful and glad.

The earth and the waters are bright —
  The skies are all beaming and mild ;
And oh ! with unmingled delight
  Thy charms fill the heart of the child !

Sweet Spring! 'twas my Maker made thee,
  And sent thee to brighten our days!
Thine aim is his glory, I see: —
  I 'll join thee in giving him praise.

My heart seems to sing like the birds ; —
  Like blossoms to open with love,
Which God will, as music and words,
  Receive for my anthem above.

THE MARINER'S ORPHAN.

That cold, faithless moon looking down on
    the wave!
  How dark grows my heart with her beam-
    ing!
And yonder she smiles on the new-covered
    grave,
  While tears drown my sight in their
    streaming.

For there lies my father, down, down in the
    deep,
  O'erwhelmed by the black, heavy billow!

And now have they borne off my mother, to
    sleep
Where damp clods of earth are her pillow.

How oft did she kneel, when that moon
    from above,
Hung mild o'er a calm, sparkling ocean ;
And lift her sweet voice in thanksgiving and
    love,
To Him of her evening devotion !

And, when into clouds all their brightness
    was cast,
With looks full of woe and imploring,
She bowed like a reed, at the rush of the
    blast ;
And prayed while the tempest was roaring.

Then, pale at the noise of the storm and the
    sea,
While tears rolled, as crystal-drops shi-
    ning,
She threw her fond arms round my brother
    and me,
Her trembling to stay by their twining.

But, oh ! when they told her the whole fatal
    tale,
  By silence her anguish was spoken;
She heard the torn bark had gone down, in
    the gale ;
  Then sunk ! for her heart-strings were
    broken.

And since, when I see the bright moon
    beaming clear,
  With stars gathered thickly around her,
I think of that night, when no ray would
    appear,
  To light the frail bark that must founder !

The sound of the waves, as they die on the
    shore,
  It fills me with sadness and sighing :
To me they bring back a dear father no
    more —
  They show me a mother, when dying.

THE DESPOILED HUMMING-BIRD.

[A Humming-Bird's nest was sent me from a distant State, still attached to the twig on which it was built. A lad, pruning a fruit-tree, lopped a branch without perceiving the nest, till he saw the small white eggs rolling out of it into a rivulet, beside which the bough fell.]

Alas ! pretty rover, thy joys are all over ;
For gone is thy soft downy nest from the
tree !
With fond bosom yearning, thou 'lt seek it
returning,
But, poor little birdie ! thy nest is with
me.

Yet, not of my doing, this deed for thy rue-
ing,
Which leaves thee in anguish thy house
to deplore :
While blessing the donor, I grieve for the
owner ;
And fain to its bough would thy building
restore.

I fancy thee coming, with light pinions hum-
ming,

Where tiny white gems thy warm cell had
    impearled ;
To mourn without measure thy rest and thy
    treasure,
    For ah ! they are gone, and that home
    was thy world.

But hadst thou forsaken the nest that was
    taken ;
    And left it, all empty and lone, on the
    bough,
With joy at receiving a house of thy leaving,
    I never had felt for thee sorrow, as now.

Whilst I can't replace it, perchance thou
    may'st trace it,
    And follow the scent of thy house from
    the tree :
Then, deem me not cruel, but come, little
    jewel !
    And find thy lost treasure in quiet with
    me.

No rudeness has marred it, nor falling has
    jarred it ;

The twig of thy choosing is under it still ;
Its thatching of mosses and inlay of flosses
Are just as composed by thy labor and
skill.

Thou only could'st form it; return, then,
and warm it
Again with thy breast, letting love banish
fear;
So, when thou art coming at eve from thy
roaming,
Thou 'lt know, my dear birdie, thy home
still is here.

The young flowerets blooming, and sweetly
perfuming
The pure air, invite thee to sip from their
store;
The honey-cup's filling! to come, then, be
willing;
I 'll shield thee from harm; thou shalt
sorrow no more!

TEACHINGS OF GOD.

He reigns on high, a glorious King,
  In ocean, earth, and air ;
He moves and governs every thing,
  For God is every where.

The waters at his bidding flow ;
  The mountain and its flower
Their majesty and beauty show,
  As traces of his power.

The lilies by the meadow rills
  Are leaning on his hand ;
And so the cedar of the hills,
  The palm and olive stand.

He formed the birds, that sport along
  On light and brilliant wing ;
And tuned them with the voice of song
  And joy, his praise to sing.

This earth is ours, so rich and fair,
  From him, who made it thus —
Who sends his angels down with care
  To minister to us.

The rainbow, with its beauteous dies,
   A pledge to man, is lent
By him, who spreads the shining skies
   Around him "as a tent."

The heavens, my child, are full of him!
   Yon radiant sun above
Is but an image, cold and dim,
   Of his great power and love.

He placed that glorious orb on high,
   In splendor there to roll,
To warm the world, to light the eye ;
   He lights and warms the soul.

And lest the night with sable shade
   That azure vault should mar,
He moved his finger there, and made,
   At every touch, a star.

With these the moon, his beaming gift,
   Here lets her lustre fall,
Our thoughts to win, our hearts to lift
   To him, who gave them all.

And he is ours — that Holy One,
  Our Father, Guide, and Friend ;
In ways untravelled by the sun,
  In love that ne'er shall end.

'Tis sweet to worship him below ;
  With his approving eye
To mark the way our spirits go
  To seek his face on high.

THE MAN AND THE MOUNTAIN.

Mountain, with thy firm old foot
  Fast beside the sea,
What was in thy keeping put, —
  Prisoned under thee ?

"Hark, and hear the shuddering ground !
  Feel it rock and quake !
Struggling fires, beneath me bound,
  Strive their chains to break."

Mountain, with a cloudy vest
  Girded o'er thy heart,

Does it pierce thine aged breast,
  When its lightnings dart?

" No :— beneath me far, the crash
  Of the bolt is felt :
Here the fiery chain and flash
  But adorn my belt."

Mountain, with a snowy crown,
  Stainless on thy brow,
Wilt thou never cast it down —
  Never, never bow?

" When the mandate I shall hear
  From my Maker's throne,
I will bow and disappear,
  Hence to be unknown."

Mountain, holding proud and high
  Thine old hoary head,
What is written on the sky,
  Thou so long hast read?

" Brighter than the stars and sun
  Shining over me,

I behold the name of ONE
Thou must die to see!"

Mountain, bold thine eloquence —
Glowing is thy speech ;
Mighty import flashes thence ;
What is it to teach ?

"Thoughts of Him, before whose breath
I shall melt away ;
While of thee, soul — spirit, death
Ne'er shall quench a ray !"

POOR MARIANNA.

Ah, poor Marianna! the scene is so bleak,
    As shivering and lonely she goes,
The wind causes half the big tear on her
        cheek,
    While round her it whistles and blows.

But why is she out with a prospect so drear,
    Beneath the cold lowering sky?
Methinks is the question which many appear
    To ask by a look or a sigh.

Of poor Marianna but sad is the tale;
    For she is the fisherman's child
Who climbed up the rock when the furious
        gale
    Turned all the black waters so wild.

While there she stood trembling and pale
        on the cliff,
    And reached forth an impotent hand,
She knew 'twas her father far out in the
        skiff,
    Hard struggling to make for the land.

Yet wild was the ocean, and sudden the
    flaw
  That kept the frail boat far from shore;
She watched the reefed sail till submerged,
    but she saw
  The boat and her father no more.

The sight was too much for her tender young
    mind;
  She shrieked and fell faint on the rock.
A ruin of reason was all that behind
  Remained, ever after the shock.

When found, and reviving, all trembling and
    pale,
  The fisherman's poor orphan child
Seemed still to behold his lone boat in the
    gale,
  'Mid billows all gloomy and wild,

Her mind is unsettled, and roving her eye,
  And sometimes she 'll harmlessly roam,
To watch the light figures in clouds on the
    sky,
  Or near the sea-rocks, in the foam.

She plucks purple berries, or bright scarlet
    haws,
In clusters that hang on the stem,
And sits by the sea-side to string them on
    straws,
Then throws in bright tresses of them.

And when the sunned waters are sleeping
    and pure,
She asks little fishes, thus drawn
So near she can see them, to nibble the lure,
To show where her father is gone.

She gathers wild flowers : — when in bou-
    quets they 're tied
She throws them far off on the wave,
And bids them go out where her poor father
    died,
And hang sweet and bright o'er his grave.

In autumn and spring, in her mantle and
    hood,
When clouds are portending a storm,
She gathers light faggots and pieces of wood,
Herself and her mother to warm.

For small is their cabin that stands by the
    sea,
  Yet far less convenient than small,
The wind and the rain in a storm making
    free
  To pour through the roof and the wall.

And oft Marianna must shake with the cold,
  For she is but scantily dressed ;
While gentle she is as the lamb in the fold,
  And harmless as dove in its nest.

And sometimes she sings such a pitiful strain,
  So sweet, and so melting — the tear
Would gush, and your heart feel strange
    pleasure and pain,
  Her music so dirge-like to hear.

Alas ! it is mournful and solemn, to see
  But ruins of reason remain,
And know the affections most holy to be
  The cause that disordered her brain.

THE WHITE COTTAGE.

Come here, my dear Loui, and laugh at thy
fear ;
The bee has not hurt thee ; so brush off the
tear,
And silence the sob, while I tell thee a tale
About the white cottage that stood in the
vale.

Around that low dwelling sweet eglantine
grew, —
Bright golden-rod, cowslip, and violets
blue ;
The raspberry-bloom, and a thousand wild
flowers
Were scattered, or clustered, or twined into
bowers.

The rich honeysuckle climbed up to its eaves ;
And near it the balm spread its high-odored
leaves ;
Green trees stood around, the wing'd warblers to house,
And robins and yellow-birds built in their
boughs.

And there the bird caroled at eve and at
    morn ;
And brought little haws they had plucked
    from the thorn,
Or wild seeds and insects they 'd gathered
    for food,
To drop in the wide-open beaks of their
    brood.

Behind the neat cot stood a snug little
    hive,
Which, had you peeped in, would have look-
    ed all alive,
At twilight, with bees in a swarm on the
    comb,
Retired for the night, at their cellular home.

But soon as the day dawned, the bees issued
    out,
To fly to the new-opened flowers all about,
Where, making their bread and their honey,
    they thought
Of winter, when none could be made, or be
    bought.

Then, back to the hive with their treasures
    they went,
Where all brought together with love and
    content,
The fruits of their labor, in one common
    store
To save for the future; and hied off for
    more.

While thus they were roving on air through
    the day,
And scattered so widely, still each knew the
    way
That led to their dear distant home, where
    at night,
They all met together in peace and de-
    light.

At peace with mankind, and content with
    their lot,
A family dwelt in that snug little cot,
While known free from envy, and ever to
    thrive,
As busy and happy as bees of their hive.

And forth from the cottage two fair little
    girls
Would run, while the fresh morning breeze
    tossed their curls,
With joy in the eye, and a smile on the lip,
To see the glad bees at the honey-cups sip.

Said one to the other, " How charming to see
The flowers yield their honey to breakfast
    the bee,
And still in their colors and fragrance re-
    main
As perfect as ever, and free from a stain."

" And then," said her sister, the brisk little
    bees
That range through the bloom of the plants
    and the trees,
And mind their own business, in constant
    employ,
Appear every moment of life to enjoy.

" They like not that others should come, it
    is true,
To meddle with them, or the course they
    pursue ;

And none ever learns they've a sting, by its
    touch,
But those who have troubled or vexed them
    too much."

The children, those sweet little sisters, were
    seen,
At morn, where the bee fed, at eve, on the
    green
The fireflies were lighting with gem after
    gem,
To bloom like twin flowers of the vale on
    their stem.

PATTY PROUD.

The figure before you is Miss Patty Proud.
Her feelings are lowery, her frown like a
    cloud,
Because proud Miss Patty can hardly en-
    dure
To come near the lowly abode of the poor.

She fears the plain floor of the humble will
    spoil
Her silk hose and shoes, and her skirt-bor-
    der soil ;
And so she goes wincing, and holds up her
    dress
So high, it were well if her heels would
    show less.

But, when she walks through the fine streets
    of the town,
She puts on fine airs, and displays her rich
    gown,
Till some who have passed her, have thought
    of the bird
Renowned for gay feathers, whose name you
    have heard.

In her thought she is trifling ; in manner, as
    vain
As that silly fowl taking pride in his train ;
And none who have marked her, will need
    to be told
That she has a heart that's unfeeling and
    cold.

I saw when she met some poor children one
day,
Who asked her for alms, she turned frown-
ing away,
And told them, "poor people must work to
be fed,
And not trouble ladies to help them to
bread."

And just as the sad little mendicants said,
Their mother was dying — their father was
dead,
She entered a store with a smooth, smiling
face,
To lay out her purse in gay ribbons and
lace.

I saw her curl up her proud lip in disdain,
Because Ellen Pitiful picked up the cane
A feeble old blind man let fall in the sand,
And placed it again in his tremulous hand.

But little does haughty Miss Patty suppose,
Of all whom she smiles on, that any one
knows

How sour she can look when she 's out of
    their sight,
And fret at the servants, if all is not right.

At home, she's unyielding, and sullen, and
    cross :
Her friends when she 's absent esteem it no
    loss ;
And some where she visits, in secret confess,
That they love her no more, though they
    dread her much less.

The truth is — Miss Patty, when young,
    never tried
To govern her temper, nor conquer her
    pride.
The passions unchecked in the heart of the
    child,
Like weeds in a garden neglected, ran wild.

They grew with her growth; with her
    strength they grew strong ;
Her head not then righted, has ever been
    wrong ;

Until she would never submit to be told
Of faults by long habit made stubborn and
bold.

And now, among all my young friends, is
there one —
A fair little girl is there under the sun,
Who 'd rise to a woman, and have it allowed,
That she is a likeness of Miss Patty Proud ?

THE YOUNG BENEFACTOR.

Overshadowed by the willow,
Near a rippling, silver stream,
Alvah has a grassy pillow :
Sweet his slumber, bright his dream !

Well may he in peace surrender
To the balmy power of sleep !
O'er a heart so warm and tender,
Angel eyes their vigils keep.

He beheld a faint wayfarer,
Old and feeble, poor and lone ;

Who appeared to have no sharer
In the woes himself must own.

Sitting on the bank that edges
Brightly this meandering brook
With a fringe of flowers and sedges,
He 'd a needy, suffering look.

Alvah viewed him, filled with pity ;
And resolved to lend him aid ;
Though from home in yonder city,
Far for wild-flowers he had strayed.

Quick he thought, his little treasure,
Given to him, and laid aside —
His bright coins to purchase pleasure —
Now might wisely be applied.

Home he ran, to seek and take them,
Out of breath, with moistened brow ;
Thinking he could never make them
Surer means of good than now.

Swift upon his way returning,
Over fen and field he ran,

Till, with feet and forehead burning,
He rejoined the poor old man.

Here, his little gift bestowing,
While a joy is in his breast
Worthy of an angel's knowing,
On the turf he sinks to rest.

Joy, too long a stranger seeming
In the wanderer's hollow eye,
Speaks his thanks, through tear-drops
    beaming,
While his words in utterance die.

There he sits, beside the sleeper,
Asking God's peculiar care —
Blessings, and a Heavenly keeper,
For a child so good and fair.

Angel guards may — thus assuming
Forms of humble souls below —
Shroud their own, too bright and bloom-
    ing
To a mortal eye to show.

Oft does He, " the King of Glory "—
    Once " the Man of Sorrows "— thus,
In the poor repeat his story,
    And the tale of Lazarus.

Now, with pleasure pure and holy,
    He regards this peaceful child,
Pillowed on a bed so lowly —
    Slumbering 'mid the flowerets wild.